Welcome to Planet Reader!

Invite your child on a journey to a wonderful, imaginative place—the limitless universe of reading! And there's no better traveling companion than you, the parent. Every time you and your child read together you send out an important message: Reading can be rewarding and *fun*. This understanding is essential to helping your child build the skills and confidence he or she needs as an emerging reader.

Here are some tips for sharing Planet Reader stories with your child:

Be open! Some children like to listen to or read the whole story and then ask questions. Some children will stop on every page with a question or a comment. Either way is fine; the most important thing is that your child feels reading is a pleasurable experience.

Be understanding! Sometimes your child might need a direct answer. If he or she points to a word and asks you to tell what it is, do so. Other times, your child may want to sound out a word or stop to figure out a sentence independently. Allow for both approaches.

Enjoy! The story and characters in this book were created especially for your child's age group. Talk about the story. Take turns reading favorite parts. Look at how the illustrations support the story and enhance the reading experience.

And most of all, enjoy your child's journey into literacy. It's one of the most important trips the two of you will ever take!

For Lovis and
for Juliet,
with many fond wishes
for nothing but net!

PIG AT PLAY

Susan Schade
& Jon Buller

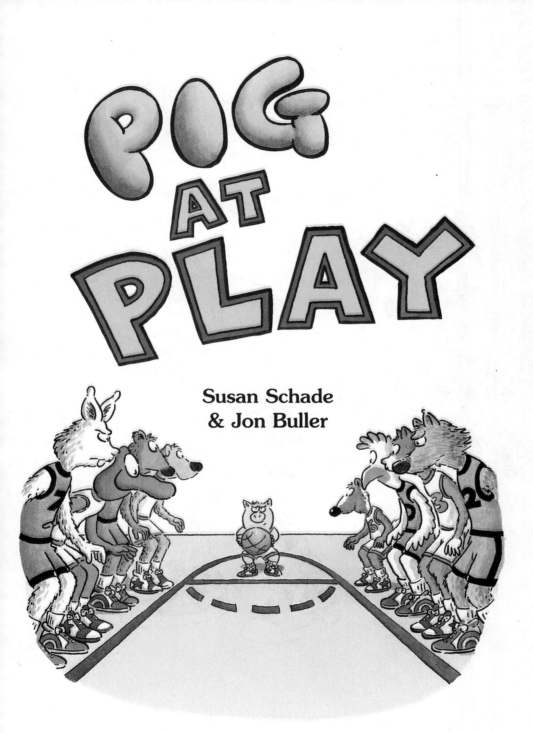

Basketball
is my sport.

They say I am . . .

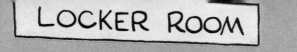

LOCKER ROOM

too fat and short.

But I don't care.
I want to play.

I practice shooting
every day.

Down at the gym
with my friend Skunk . . .

I face the fact
I cannot dunk.

Instead I practice
shooting threes.

And learn to dribble
through my knees.

We both try out,
but Coach says no.
Skunk can play, but . . .

I'm too slow.

I practice more.
I lift. I pump.
I get strong arms.

I run.

I jump.

Coach sees me train.
Is this a dream?

My work pays off.
I make the team!

It's my first game.
I'm number eight.

I'm on the bench.
I sit and wait.

We're down by ten.
It's second half.
Coach puts me in.

The others laugh.

They think they're tough.
They don't scare me.

I steal the ball.

I sink a three.

Hooray for Pig!
Now I am hot.
I dribble down.

I make the shot!

I cannot miss!

We win the game!

Basketball Pig is my name!